. . . for parents an.

MW00904326

With a large percentage of families affected by alcoholism, countless young children are being faced with the trauma of coping with an alcoholic parent.

Sometimes My Mom Drinks Too Much, through its simple narrative and dialogue, illustrates the impact that a parent's alcoholism can have on the entire family, particularly the child. Whether at home or in school, Maureen is constantly struggling to cope with the effects of her mother's alcoholism.

This story also suggests where children like Maureen can turn for help — to relatives, friends, and teachers who can counter a child's feelings of shame, fear, bewilderment, and rejection.

By explaining to Maureen that her mother's new and strange behavior is caused by illness — a familiar concept — and by enlisting Maureen's aid, the father helps the child to face the problem and channel her thoughts into a positive direction.

Children in a situation similar to Maureen's will be able to identify with her and draw comfort from the message that they are not alone. They, and the children who merely know someone like Maureen, will find their understanding of alcoholism expanded through the reading of this story.

T. H. NEIDENGARD, M.D.
CHIEF OF SERVICE, CABRINI
ALCOHOLISM PROGRAM
CABRINI MEDICAL CENTER, A NEW
YORK UNIVERSITY MEDICAL
CENTER AFFILIATE
NEW YORK, NEW YORK

Helen Krull is a counselor at Chicago Lakeshore
Alcoholism Institute for Recovery, an affiliate of
Chicago Lakeshore Hospital in Illinois. Kevin Kenny is
the author of twenty-one books for children.

Trade Edition published 1992 © Steck-Vaughn Company

Copyright © 1991 Steck-Vaughn Company

Copyright © 1980, Raintree Publishers Limited
Partnership

Library of Congress Number: 80-14515

    11 12   93 92

Library of Congress Cataloging in Publication Data

Kenny, Kevin.
  Sometimes my mom drinks too much.

  SUMMARY: Her feelings toward her alcoholic mother
vary as Maureen struggles to understand her mother's
illness.
  (1. Alcoholism — Fiction. 2. Mothers and daughters
— Fiction.) I. Krull, Helen, joint author.
II. Cogancherry, Helen. III. Title.
PZ7.K3964So   (Fic)   80-14515
ISBN 0-8172-1366-X   hardcover library binding
ISBN 0-8114-7159-4   softcover binding

SOMETIMES MY MOM DRINKS TOO MUCH

by Kevin Kenny and Helen Krull

illustrated by Helen Cogancherry

introduction by T. H. Neidengard, M.D.

RSVP

RAINTREE STECK-VAUGHN
P U B L I S H E R S
The Steck-Vaughn Company

Austin, Texas

I don't like it when my mom drinks too much. She doesn't seem like Mom after she's been drinking alcohol. It spoils all the fun she and Dad and I used to have when we were a *real* family.

I remember when we used to do things together — just the three of us. Mom and Dad would be smiling at each other. And both of them would be smiling at me.

Neither one of them smiles very much anymore. And I never know what to expect from Mom.

Sometimes I'm afraid of her.

One day she yelled at me for not having my homework done. "Maureen," she said, "you're not getting any dinner until you do your homework!"

She was so mad that I was afraid to tell her I didn't *have* any homework that day.

Sometimes she confuses me.

Later that night, she told me she was sorry about not letting me have any dinner. She took me out for a pizza and a milk shake. I liked the dinner, but I was still confused.

Other times, she embarrasses me.

Once we had a big concert at my school. My dad is the orchestra conductor. I play the clarinet. We were both very excited.

Mom was late for the concert. Then she couldn't find her seat. Other people had to help her.

When it was over, she clapped and clapped. People began to turn around and stare at her.

Then my friend Yoshi whispered to me, "What's the matter with your mom? Is she drunk?"

The way Yoshi said *drunk*, it sounded terrible.

Sometimes I feel sorry for Mom.
She has a job working with computers. I
know she likes it, but some mornings she
feels too sick from drinking to go to work.

Then my dad has to call her company. "Mrs. Kelly won't be going to work today," he'll say. "She has the flu."

I try to help Dad take care of Mom, even though I know she doesn't have the flu. It makes me sad when Dad has to lie to her boss.

Sometimes Mom disappoints me.

Once Dad and I made a special dinner. He cooked steaks on the grill. I cut up vegetables for a big salad. We bought things to make fancy ice-cream sundaes for dessert.

But Mom was very late coming home that night. We were already eating our sundaes, and her steak was cold. She wasn't hungry anyway, so we fed her food to the dog.

No one was smiling that night.

Oh, sometimes Mom still smiles, but mostly at things I don't think are funny. She smiled a lot at my birthday party this year.

She was carrying my birthday cake to the table where I was sitting with my friends. Suddenly she fell. The cake smashed all over the floor.

Mom burst out laughing. My friends laughed too. But I didn't.

Neither did Yoshi. I could tell she was thinking, *Your mom is drunk, isn't she?*

After that party, I started feeling that everything bad that was happening to me was all her fault. I was mad.

"Why does Mom hate me?" I asked Dad one day. "And what does Yoshi mean when she says Mom's drunk? Is being drunk what makes Mom hate me?"

Dad put his arm around me. "Mom doesn't hate you," he said slowly. "She has a sickness, like measles or chicken pox. It's called alcoholism."

"A sickness about alcohol?" I asked.

Dad nodded. "It makes her drink more than she means to. It makes her act strangely. That's what Yoshi means by drunk. Mom's sickness makes her act differently than she wants to toward you."

"But *I'm* not any different," I said.

"I know, Maureen. You have to try to understand that the way Mom acts has nothing to do with you. She's sick inside of herself."

I tried to understand. But it's hard, especially since sometimes I have the feeling that Dad hates me too.

Sometimes he yells at me for not doing my homework or feeding the dog or setting the table.

I think he yells at me sometimes because he's upset with Mom.

Then why doesn't he yell at her?

I spend a lot of time with my friends. That makes me feel less alone.

My teachers are very nice to me too, especially after the night of my school's first parent-teacher conference.

When Mom and Dad left to go to the school, I could tell Mom had been drinking.

I was in bed when they came home, but I could hear part of a big fight Dad had with Mom.

One of my teachers, Ms. Williams, talked to me after school the next day. I told her about my mom's drinking.

Ms. Williams asked me to come and talk to her any time I want. Sometimes she calls our house too. My dad takes the phone into another room and talks to her.

Lately Mom has been staying home from her job more and more.

One day, I came home from school and no one was there. On the table was a note from Dad: "Don't worry. I'll be home in time for dinner."

It got later and later. I *did* get worried.

Finally Dad came home. He was alone, and he looked very tired.

"Where's Mom?" I asked.

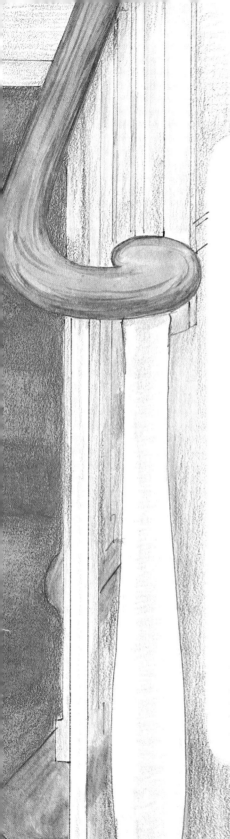

He sat down. "Your mom is in a special hospital for a few weeks," he said.

"You mean, you — you sent her away?"

"It wasn't my idea," he said. "It was hers and her boss's. They think that this hospital will help her. I thought about it for a long time, and I decided they were right. You and I can take care of each other till she gets back."

"But, Dad, when she gets back — will she be all right? Will she still be sick from so much drinking?"

"I don't know," he said. "I could say that she'll be all right. But the real answer is that no one knows for sure. When she comes back, she will be going to meetings and seeing people who can help her get better. You and I have to help too. So, with all of us helping, there's a very good chance she will be all right. But you and I always have to remember that she has a sickness that's not our fault. We can help her get well, but she has to help herself too."

"I'll help," I promised.

"I know you will," Dad said, and he smiled.

"Should I start setting the table?" I asked.

Dad hugged me. "Why don't you call up Yoshi? I'll take both of you out for a hamburger. How does that sound?"

"Okay!" I said and ran to the phone.